It had been a wonderful warm summer for the kids at Camp Victory but a severe thunderstorm rushed up on them one evening. Camp Director, Mr. Romano called out to the Youth Counselors, "Get everyone to their cabins right away! I just checked the weather report, a big storm is coming in!"

The wind picked up quickly and the tree tops swayed with a loud SWOOSH! The kids were starting to panic, but the Youth Counselors had it under control. First they helped the kids with wheelchairs and crutches then it started to sprinkle as the sky grew dark. Joshua, the oldest of the Youth Counselors called out, "Help your neighbors who need a hand, let's get everyone to shelter right away!"

Matthew grabbed his buddy by the arm, "Hey Panjay! Shawna?! She needs help getting back to the cabins!"

Panjay, "I see her over there. Better hurry, the storm is coming in fast!"

Mathew, "I'll find Beth and walk her to shelter. Let's see who gets back first!"

Across the playground their friend Beth was pushing Shawna in her wheelchair as fast as she could go. Shawna had her hand raised up, shouting, "You're doing great Beth, a little to the left! Whoa! Just missed that big rock. Faster Beth, I'm getting wet!" The sound of their shrieks of laughter filled the air.

Matthew and Panjay ran over to the girls to help, then heavy rain started pouring down.

Matthew called out, "Hey! Lets get under that gazebo, it's the closest shelter!" Matthew picked up Beth and ran her to shelter. Panjay grabbed the back of Shawna's wheelchair and pushed as fast as he could. A bold of lightening rang out of the sky, BOOM!

Under the gazebo, sopping wet they all started laughing. Shawna grabbed Beth's hand, "That was fun! Let's go back into the rain!"

Suddenly a tremendous lighting flash lit up the sky and a thunder clap boomed through the campground. All of them screamed and huddled together. A moment later they looked at each other dripping with rain and burst out laughing.

Panjay said to himself, "I love rain."

The next morning Mr. Romano sounded the morning bell that calls everyone to the Mess Hall for breakfast. When everyone came out of their cabins they were shocked at how much damage they saw in the camp ground. Many of the facilities were damaged, even the electricity was out in some places. Everyone was really upset, "At least you are all safe, that's the important thing." Said Mr. Romano.

Mr. Romano directed the Youth Counselors to get the kids fed. They all ate in silence as Mr. Romano paced back and forth rubbing his bearded chin. Finally he stopped and spoke to the campers, "In all my years running Camp Victory, I've never seen a storm do so much damage. Adding up the cost for all the repairs is something I cannot afford. I really hate to do this but I'm going to have to call your parents to come pick you all up and close the camp. I'll have to refund their money too."

A horrible gasp came out of everyone including the Youth Counselors. Nobody expected this kind of reaction from the Director of Camp Victory, but the damages were so bad and everyone understood the terrible truth.

Beth put her head in her hands, "That's it, summer is ruined!"

Shawna put her arm around Beth to comfort her, "Don't cry Beth, it's going to be okay."

"I'm bummed! This was going to be a great summer." Matthew just shrugged and frowned, what else could he do? Sanjay pouted, "I don't like closing down camp for summer."

To everyone's surprise, two women walked into the Mess Hall, both professionally dressed. "Pardon the intrusion but I noticed you have a lot of damage in your camp ground. Must have been from that terrible storm we just had. We came by to see if everyone was alright."

Looking confused, Mr. Romano approached them, putting his hand out in greeting, " I'm Mr. Romano, Director here at Camp Victory. Are either of you relatives of the kids here? May I ask your names?"

"Hillary Rosenberg, entrepreneur at large. This is my secretary, Ms. Lashawndra Lopez." Both the women passed by Mr. Romano to step in front of the campers at their tables. Mr. Romano, feeling awkward, said, "I'm sorry ladies, this is a very bad time to talk but…May I ask what you are doing here?"

Ms Rosenberg ruffled her curly black hair and adjusted her circular red glasses, "Mr.…?" "Romano."

"Mr. Romano, I represent a charitable organization that helps out organizations like yours in times of need. You clearly have extensive damage to Camp….?

Mr. Romano, "Camp Victory, for kids with dis…"

"Camp Victory! Yes, well it's Camp Loser now, isn't it Romano?" She said in a snarky tone while admiring the gloss on her nails.

The campers and Youth Counselors grumble, offended by this insult.

Mr. Romano, "Now Mrs. Rosenberg…

"MIZZ ROSENBERG!" She said with a cold glare.

"Oh, uh, Ms Rosenberg," the Director continued, "that kind of talk is unnecessary, we always bounce back here at Camp Victory and…"

Ms Rosenberg bursts out laughing loudly, shoots a glare at Ms. Lopez who then bursts out in laughter. "Oh that's quaint Mr. Ro-ma-no. Don't get your spaghetti in a knot. Listen, we are here to help. We want to offer to fix all the damage so you can keep Camp Victory open this summer."

All the campers and Youth Counselors sat up and listened anxiously.

Mr. Romano scratches his beard and looks at her sideways. "And what do you want in return?"

"Mr. Romano, if you will have a look here." Ms Lopez steps forward, opening her briefcase and pulling out pen and paper.

"If you sign here, we'll cover all the repairs and Camp Victory will be better than ever."

Looking out over the anxious faces of all the kids, all of them overcoming challenges with their disabilities, knowing they waited all year for Camp Victory, Mr. Romano's heart grew heavy. He then looked at all the Youth Counselors and realized he would have to let them all go and close the camp permanently if he could not repair the campground. Slowly, he picked up the pen and signed the paper.

Ms Rosenberg, "Fantastic! We'll have mechanics come to fix the damages, they will be here within the hour. I will be organizing a fundraiser through the local news to help cover the costs of repairs."

Mr. Romano, looking puzzled, said, "But you said you would cover the costs."

Ms Lopez, looking down her nose at Mr. Romano, "It clearly states in subtext H-14, and I quote, Camp Director shall have campers put on a show, bake sale or other events for a fundraiser to help pay repair costs from Rosenberg Interests LLC."

Mr. Romano's patience was running thin when Sally the Youth Counselors saw what was happening and stepped in, "No problem! The Youth Counselors are very musical and we put on shows with the campers all the time." Ramone, another Youth Counselor jumps up behind her, "Yeah, we can do the songs we play around the campfire at night. We got you covered, Mr. Romano."

Ms Rosenberg spins around and walks briskly to the door, "No time for small talk, must get marketing our big fundraiser. Be sure to keep your kids away from the damaged sites, the repairmen will take care of everything." With a slam of the door, they were gone as quickly as they came, Mr. Romano turned back to the campers with a look of disbelief on his face, "Well kids, looks like summer is not cancelled!"

HURRAY, they all cheered!

Matthew was excited, he turned to Beth, Panjay and Shawna, "WOO-HOO! You hear that!?

What a stroke of good luck!"

Shawna shook her head and said quietly, "I can't see her but I got a bad feeling about that lady."

Beth patted her on the back, "Oh come on, don't be a downer Shawna. Let's take a picture of everyone here to remember this moment." When Beth reached into her compartment on her wheelchair a look of horror came over her face, "Oh no! My phone! It's gone."

Matthew, "Could it have fallen out when we were rushing to get out of the rain?" Beth, "That's very possible."

Panjay, "Let's trace our steps back, we gotta give it a chance."

While the four were out looking for Shawna's phone, they noticed lots of car tracks around the damaged areas at the camp. "That's weird," Panjay said, "How could there be car tracks here? It's not even close to the road."

Matthew, "The rain made it really muddy so it's easy to see where the tracks came from." Shawna, "Do you see my phone anywhere? Oh wait! I forgot, I slipped it in my jacket pocket,

here it is."

They all laughed, "You silly Billy!" said Beth. Panjay followed "We are all out here in the mud for nothing, but that's okay, I love mud! Let's go on a mud adventure!"

Just then Panjay ran off following the car tracks. They chased after him, "Hey wait up!" Matthew cried, "I can't push Shawna's wheelchair that well in this goop!" Shawna got out her phone and started snapping pictures of her friends chasing around in the mud.

"Wait a minute" Matthew paused, "these tracks lead to the next place where the damage is. And look over there, the tracks go from one damaged spot to the next!"

Beth crossed her arms as she often does when deep in thought, "Maybe it was that Rosenberg lady assessing all the damages. She probably had to do that to figure out how much it would cost." Shawna took pictures of car tracks and the damaged areas, "That's weird, there's no tree branches around here, and how could that trampoline be ripped unless something cut through it?"

Panjay replied, "Maybe it got hit by lightning."

Mathew pointed out, "Yeah but look at those broken windows, you'd think there'd be tree bark and leaves all over the place, maybe scratches on the windowsill... but nothing."

Shawna, "HA! You guys are PAR-A-NOID! You going to start your own Storm Hunter show?" They all laughed, Shawna continued, "Who cares how it got broken, we got our camp back for the summer, that's all that matters."

Later that day many trucks arrived with workers and equipment to fix the camp. There was a lot of noise and commotion as they fixed up Camp Victory. Inside the Mess Hall, the Youth Counselors were leading the campers through many campfire songs while others were helping campers to make decorations for the fundraiser. Everyone was in a good mood, but Mr.

Romano seemed unusually quiet, watching everyone from the corner.

"Hey! Look everyone, look outside!" Matthew saw that six different news channels arrived following a black limousine. The camera men all got out and started taking photos of Ms Rosenberg and Ms Lewis coming out of the limousine. Ms Rosenberg begins to lead the reporters around the campground telling them about how badly Camp Victory needs donations, "We are holding a grand fundraiser to help the kids get their camp back, won't you help us?"

Soon the Youth Counselors put on a fabulous show leading the campers in song. Mathew, Beth, Panjay and Shawna all sang to the top of their lungs and had a wonderful time. Many parents came for this special event and there were snacks and drinks afterwards

for everyone to celebrate. Ms Rosenberg was busy counting the donations and working on her calculator when the news channels packed up their equipment and drove off.

The following day Camp Victory was back in business, Youth Counselors were leading Arts and Crafts, Sports, Games and other activities for the disabled campers. The glow of happiness filled the air, except for Mr. Romano. He seemed unusually quiet.

"Why the long face Mr. Romano?" Asked Shawna.

"Oh, nothing really. You children go enjoy yourselves." Mr. Romano looked away to hide the sad look on his face.

Beth chimed in, "I can't see your face but I can hear in your voice that something is not right. What could be bothering you Mr. Romano? We just had a huge fundraiser and we are all on the news now!"

Mr. Romano smiled warmly, "Aw, that's kind of you Beth. You've got a good heart. It's just silly adult stuff. You all go enjoy this beautiful day, I'll be in my office."

As he walked away, Matthew looked at the others, "Who's thinking what I'm thinking?" Beth replied, "Yep, we'd better investigate."

Shawna, "OK, Beth you put your ear to Mr. Romano's door, Panjay, you be the lookout.

Mathew, if anyone comes along we'll slow them down."

Panjay, "Cool! We are like the Camp Victory detectives! I like this game!"

As the kids went on their investigation, they noticed Ramone and Sally, two of the Youth Counselors, go into Mr. Romano's office. Beth and Mathew scooted in silently behind them and pressed their ears to the door.

"Hello Mr. Romano, you wanted to see us?" Sally started the conversation.

"Take a seat Sally and Ramone, what I have to say is very difficult. You see, with my contract with Rosenberg Interests, I have to make some cutbacks."

Ramone spoke up, "B-but we just had a huge fundraiser, where did all that money go?"

Mr. Romano, looked down and folded his hands, "It looks like that money goes into a bank account and cannot be touched until all the damages have been paid for."

Sally was outraged, "But that lady said SHE would pay for the damages! I don't get it."

Mr. Romano pulled out a copy of the agreement he signed. "I have to apologize, my hands were tied. I either signed the contract or Camp Victory would be closed and no one would have a summer camp, no one would have a summer job."

"Mr. Romano, I understand, it's a difficult decision but... the kids come first."

Mr. Romano stood up and started pacing the room, "Look, it pains me to let you go but I'll have you back next year. I don't know how many more counselors I'll have to let go. I have to pay back to Ms. Rosenberg for the repairs, I can't afford staff for this summer. I'll have to let go of more staff each week."

Sally and Ramone stood up, shook his hand and offered their sympathies. As they left, Ramone turned back, "We'll pray for you Mr. Ramone, and for all of Camp Victory."

Mr. Ramone gives a warm smile and waves them goodbye.

Mathew pulled Beth aside, hiding around the corner, "Oh my gosh! Did you hear that?!" "Shhhhhh Matthew, they are going to hear you." Protested Beth putting her finger up to her lips. She gave him a light hit from her cane and a scolding face.

"This is crazy, we've got to tell the other Counselors." Matthew said, "What good is Camp Victory without it's counselors?"

Beth was busy thinking, "MIZZ Rosenberg isn't really a humanitarian. She just pretends to be one to use people less fortunate to make money. This was all a trick. Poor Mr. Romano."

Panjay wheeled Shawna over quickly but quietly. Shawna leaning forward whispered loudly, "What did you hear? What's the scoop?"

Matthew leaned into the close circle they formed, "Look, somethings up here. First the damage to the camp looks suspicious, now Mr. Romano is letting Youth Counselors go..."

"What?!" Panjay blurted out loudly. Shawna quickly put her hand over his mouth, "You're kidding me. That makes no sense, what about the fundraiser? I heard they made thousands."

Beth, "Looks like all the money is going to the..." using air quotes "HUMANITARIAN who saved the day."

Panjay and Shawna simultaneously, "No way!"

They both slap their own mouths shut for being so loud. "Yes way." Matthew interjects.

"Hang on" Shawna pulls out her phone from it's pouch, "I've got pictures of those damages..." Beth adds, "Do you have pictures of the car tracks? I have an idea."

Shawna scrolls through her phone and sure enough there are close ups of the car tracks, "Yeah, but how does that help us?"

Matthew starts to put the picture together, "Lets match the pattern of those tracks to Rosenberg's car."

Panjay adds, "Whoa! You mean..." They all look at him, "Yep."

Panjay exclaims, "This is a job for the Camp Victory Detectives!"

The kids sneak around the campground to the parking lot, they find Ms Rosenberg's car and look at the tires. Panjay notices, "Gee, for a fancy car, it sure is muddy."

Shawna holds up her photos of the tracks to the car wheel, Beth asks, "Does it match?" Shawna's eyes widened, "Whoa! They do match."

Mathew calls out anxiously, "Hey, look in the backseat! Why is there a baseball bat in there?" Panjay, "I like baseball."

Matthew, "Funny, she doesn't strike me as the baseball type. Get it!? STRIKE me... as the baseball... type."

Shawna, "A little young for the Dad jokes, aren't you Matt?"

Beth, "Shawna, do you think the damage on the cabins look like they came from a baseball bat?"

"I dunno? Let's see..." They all gathered around Shawna. Mathew leaned in to get a closer look, "Well I'll be darned! We just solved our first mystery. Those are definitely marks from a baseball bat."

Panjay is angry now, "Bad bad bad!"

Shawna puts her hand on Pajeet's shoulder, "Hey, calm down, they are going to have another Fundraiser in a few days. I'm sure they'll make enough money to pay off the repairs and..."

Beth interjected, "I may have the use of your eyes, but you still don't see. This lady, this entrepreneur... she's a scammer!"

Matthew, "Yeah, she should go to jail for vandalizing our camp! Tricking Romano into paying her for damages she caused, that's just evil."

Beth, "Create the problem and sell the solution."

Shawna's eyes widened, "Who could think of such a diabolical plan?"

Matthew, "Listen, I think I've got an idea that will turn everything around. It's totally crazy but..." Beth sarcastically, "You? Crazy ideas? Nooooo."

They all snickered and huddled in close to listen.

Later, during dinner in the Mess Hall, Ms Rosenberg steps up with a megaphone. "Listen up people! Public announcement!"

The campers all clamped their hands over their ears, and some of the kids shouted, "Stop!"

Patrick, a Youth Counselor stepped up quickly to Ms Rosenberg, "Ma'am! Please don't do that, some of our campers are very sensitive to loud noises. You can just speak normally, I'll do sign language for those who are hearing impaired."

"Fine!" Rosenberg hands the megaphone to Ms Lopez, who fumbles and drops it on her toe, KLONK!

"Listen carefully my darlings. Next week we are having the inter-camp Special Kids Olympics and I am making it a major fundraiser for Camp Victory. There will be even more news channels here, you are all going to be famous!"

The campers were so quiet you could hear a pin drop. Rosenberg paused and looked at them confused, "Don't you want to be famous? Well, it doesn't matter, what matters is that you listen very carefully. Now, in order for Camp Victory to be successful, I'm going to have to ask you to LOSE the sporting competitions."

Everyone responded together, "Whaaaaat?!"

"Hold your horses little ones, Ms Rosenberg knows what's best. I've been in this business a looooong time, haven't I Ms Lopez?" The two of them give each other a wink.

"Don't you see, people don't want to help winners, they want to help losers! Just imagine Americans watching this story in their comfy little living rooms, they see all these poor, helpless handicapped kids struggling to make it across the finishing line, all sad-faced. Mr. and Mrs.

America will say, 'Where's my wallet?! These kids need help!!'"

Ms Lopez murmured something under her breath and they both snickered.

Panjay shouts from the back of the Mess Hall, "Camp Victory is for winners!" Everyone cheered loudly and went into their camp's song; "Victory, Victory! That's our chant, We always win, we never say can't! Victory, Victory, And-a-big-Heave Ho! Nothing can stop us, now LET'S GO!" The hall erupted in shouts and applause. Patrick turned to Ms Rosenberg with a grin, "It's gonna be hard getting them to lose, they have an unstoppable spirit."

Ms. Rosenberg stepped into the middle of the Mess Hall and beamed a spiteful glare around the room, "Oh, isn't that quaint. How delightful that you have your little cheerleader chants. That will look great on camera. Now darlings, try to understand; SYMPATHY SELLS! We need sympathy from the viewers at home otherwise they won't send any money for our big fundraiser. Understand? You can do that for me...uh, the Camp, can't you? I would hate to have to leave the rest of the storm damage unfinished."

The campers were stone cold quiet, "I'd expect a little more gratitude for the person who is fixing up your camp. I'm only trying to help!"

You could hear a pin drop. "Alright, I know you are the best and so why not let another group of handicapped kids win this year, huh? That would be nice wouldn't it? You want to be nice, don't you?"

Shawna spoke up, "Ms Rosenberg? Where will the fundraiser money go?"

"Well, to the camp darling, of course. Wouldn't you all like a new swimming pool? How about some video games? Or maybe you'd like ice cream everyday?"

The campers chatted among themselves and this was enough to reassure Rosenberg so she and Ms Lopez turned around and headed for the exit.

Beth, Matthew, Shawna and Panjay were fit to be tied. Their faces grew flush with anger.

Panjay tried to stand up but Beth pulled him down to his seat. "Cool down buddy, our time will come."

A week had passed and the big day arrived, Camp Victory was decked out with all sorts of decorations; American flags, streamers, and lights that the campers put up. Music filled the air as busses arrived from other camps for disabled kids. The media sets their cameras and does interviews of several families attending. Many of the Youth Counselors who had to be let go returned to cheer on the campers of Camp Victory, the reunions were cheerful.

Shawna checked to see her phone was fully charged and started to follow Ms Rosenberg and Ms Lopez. Shawna pulled up in her wheelchair behind them. Mr. Romano approached and asked, "Hey Shawna, why aren't you in the competitions? You've got the fastest wheels in the West!"

Shawna blushed and giggled, "Thanks Mr. Romano! I'm a little under the weather today so I'm just going to enjoy the sporting events."

"Well I hope you feel better, I've gotta get the games started." Mr. Romano rushed off. Shawna pulled her phone out and opened the recording app.

The air was bristling with excitement as all the parents of each camp were seated around the event. The Olympic music was blasting over the loudspeakers as Mr. Romano stepped up to the podium with a microphone, "Ladies and gentlemen! Thank you for attending the annual Camp Victory Special Kids Olympics! This year promises to be very exciting, we have top athletes competing for the gold ribbons of each sport. We are very proud of our young athletes, they have trained hard this summer! Thank you to all the camp counselors who helped and thanks to all the families attending today!"

Just then, Ms Rosenberg yelled to Mr. Romano from her seat, "DON'T FORGET TO THANK THEM FOR THEIR FINANCIAL SUPPORT!"

People around her were surprised at this but Mr. Romano quickly took back their attention, "Yes and we are very grateful for your generous support. Now! Let the games begin!"

Panjay lined up with the other runners at the 100 Yard Dash, kicking off the Track and Field events. He thought about how Mr. Romano was coerced into signing a deal with that weird woman with the weird glasses. He thought about all the broken cabins and other damage she and her minion caused in the park. He thought about the staff counselors that lost their summer jobs and missed them. Panjay knew he was not likely to win the race, he's not as athletic as the other kids but all these things really boiled his blood, his spirit was on fire for victory!

BANG! The starting gun went off and Sanjay exploded onto the track like a rocket. First he passed, one, then another, then another. Quickly the yellow ribbon at the finishing line was zooming up to him and just in time he passed the last runner and broke the ribbon! The crowd went wild, what an upset! Camp Victory was cheering for him in support but everyone was impressed by the power of his spirit. They lifted him up, with some effort and sang their camp song.

Ms Rodriguez leans towards Ms Rosenberg, " Um, Ma'am, I think that was the one that spoke back at you in the mess hall."

Ms Rosenberg, took off her glasses, wiped them clean and put them back on. Her eyes were laser focused on Sanjay, "Hmmmm, yes, indeed it is. This one is a troublemaker."

Ma Rodriguez continued, "Well, it's only the first event of the day, and he's only one person.

The others won't follow."

Throughout the day the kids competed in various sports and games. Although the competitions were quite hard, many of them were won by Camp Victory kids. Each time one of the kids from Camp Victory won an event, Ms Rosenberg would get a little more angry. Even her assistant was getting more and more angry. The cheers from the audience drowned out anything those two were saying to each other but Shawna was staying close and getting a lot of conversation recorded.

Matthew's favorite sport is soccer, he's very good at it. He scored the winning goal that made Camp Victory the top soccer team at this year's games. The crowd roared when he won the final goal but Ms Rosenberg only sunk into her chair. She realized that these kids were not going for her plan.

"Hey Rodriguez!" Ms Rosenberg yelled over the crowd's applause. "Yes Ma'am!"

"Isn't that one of the kids sitting with the troublemaker in the mess hall?" Rosenberg glared. "Hmmm, yes, yes it is! Another troublemaker. I'll find out their names and get a report for you

Ms Rosenberg."

The Girl's Judo competition began as Mr. Romano called the competitors out on the padded floor. These girls have been training all year and were very good. Beth was a natural at Judo because her blindness trained her other senses to be stronger than other people. She could hear the shuffle of her opponent's feet and feel the force they were pushing on her. With this she could easily swing them into position for a good Judo flip.

One by one the competition narrowed down the girls from all the different camps. The competition was intense and gave the audience a great deal of entertainment. When the final challengers were decided, it was Ramona Ramirez versus Beth. Last year Ramona defeated Beth, a shudder of fear rushed through her body knowing that she was going up against her strongest foe, but last year she did not make it to the finals either. She had learned from her mistakes, listened closely to her instructor and sacrificed a lot of play time to improve her Judo skills.

Most of the audience knew Ramona was the champion last year so they expected her to win again this year. Beth calmed down and practiced a little meditation to focus her mind and control her fear. She went onto the matt and the referee blow the whistle. At first Ramona was very aggressive, grabbing and tugging Beth's uniform. Beth kept her breath steady and 'listened' to her opponent's movements. SWOOP-BAM! She flipped Ramona to the mat!

Round 2, round 3, SWOOP-BAM, SWOOP-BAM, SWOOP-BAM! Camp Victory jumped for joy, cheering wildly for Beth, the new Girl's Judo champion.

The end of the long but wonderful day came and the winner of this year's Special Kid's Olympics was announced by the National Special Kid's Olympics officer.

"Ladies and Gentlemen, thank you for joining us this year at these very special games, for these very special children. It's been a really exciting event this summer, everyone who played put in their all and we honor all of the players for their dedication and hard work.

It's my pleasure to announce this year's winner of the Special Kid's Olympics, a man we all know and love, MR. ROMANO OF CAMP VICTORY!"

The crowd roared with applause, the campers and counselors of Camp Victory jumped and danced and gave each other High Fives while Mr. Romano stepped up on the stage and received the gold cup for Camp Victory. He was glowing with happiness, his curly mustache smile stretching from ear to ear. He stepped up to the microphone and spoke.

"Thank you so much for this. I accept this on behalf of all the kids and counselors at Camp Victory! To the parents of our campers, your love and support for these yearly competitions are so very important. We all have our struggles and limitations in life, some greater than others but if we come together to help eachother out, it makes us all better people, and helps form stronger communities."

The audience clapped and cheered some more. Panjay, Beth, Matthew and Shawna came together in a group hug, "We did it, we did it!" Suddenly, Shawna looked over her shoulder to see what Ms Rosenberg and Ms Lopez were doing. They were gone!

Suddenly the cheerful mood was shattered by the noise of two people shouting. The entire audience, campers and staff saw two women going crazy, making a horrible noise. No one could believe their eyes. Ms Rosenberg and Ms Lopez were smashing the food tables with baseball bats!

Mr. Romano shouted, "What in blue blazes is going on here!?" Everyone rushed over to the scene, Shawna quickly turned her phone on and caught the scene.

Matthew said to his friends, "Now is the time to tell Mr. Romano what we found out!" Beth said, "Can someone tell me what's going on??"

Sanjay replied, "Crazy hair woman and friend are smashing up the tables with all the food! Oh no! All those desserts! We've got to save the cakes and cookies!"

Beth grabbed Sanjay's sleeve, "Hold on buddy! Let's let the adults handle it. Shawna…" "Two steps ahead of you Beth, I'm getting all this on video."

Mr. Romano had security call the police while the counselors got everyone to safety. Matthew ran up to Romano, "Mr. Romano! We have some videos to show you. We can prove that Ms Rosenberg was the one who caused all the damage to the camp!"

Mr. Romano's eyes widened, "Whaaaat?!"

"Yes Sir! Shawna has it all on video and we matched the tire tracks and found the baseball bats and we heard you talking with the counselors and, and…" Matthew was out of breath.

Mr. Romano put his hand on Matthew's shoulder, "Calm down there buddy, police are almost here, we'll get to the bottom of this!"

Before long, the two swindlers were put in handcuffs and put into the back of a police car while the kids made their report to the police and gave them all the video documentation. Mr. Romano was very impressed with their detective skills and very grateful for all their help.

"You four are the pride of the entire camp. With your combined efforts you somehow figured out that Camp Victory was being scammed! I don't know what kind of person could put so much time and effort into lying and cheating others, especially people who are kind and trying to do something good for the world. The lesson here is that kind people have to take extra effort to protect themselves, and learn how to see the wolf in sheep's clothing."

The counselors came over, they were all interested in learning how the four heroes cracked the case and saved Camp Victory. All the counselors who had lost their jobs were particularly interested.

Ramone told the kids, "Wow, I'm so impressed! You guys are the BEST!"

Mr. Romano followed, "I think this calls for a special celebration. While we are having our victory party, I'd like you four to come up and talk to the campers about how you saved our summer."

Beth replied, "Gee, I've never given a speech before, I guess I could as long as I've got my friends to help out."

Shawna, "Besties to the end Beth!"

Matthew, "We are the best of the Besties!" Everyone laughed together and drew a great big sigh of relief.

Panjay smiled, "I like being the best."

Camp Victory

Written and illustrated by
Don Jackson
djacksonart.wixsite.com/books

ISBN# 978-1-945423-29-29-1